DeDe
Takes Charge!

BY JOHANNA HURWITZ

Aldo Applesauce
Aldo Ice Cream
Baseball Fever
Busybody Nora
The Hot and Cold Summer
The Law of Gravity
A Llama in the Family
Much Ado About Aldo
New Neighbors for Nora
Nora and Mrs. Mind-Your-Own-Business
Once I Was a Plum Tree
The Rabbi's Girls
Rip-Roaring Russell
School Spirit
Superduper Teddy
Tough-Luck Karen

Johanna Hurwitz

DeDe
Takes Charge!

illustrated by Diane de Groat

Morrow Junior Books
New York

Printed in the United States of America.

14 13 12 11 10 9 8

Library of Congress Cataloging in Publication Data
Hurwitz, Johanna.   DeDe takes charge!
Summary: A year after her father has left home for good, fifth-grader DeDe helps her mother cope with the realities of life after divorce.
1. Children's stories, American. [1. Divorce—Fiction. 2. Single-parent family—Fiction] I. De Groat, Diane, ill. II. Title.
PZ7.H9574De   1984   [Fic]   84-9085
ISBN 0-688-03853-0

Contents

One

Noise in the Night

It was two o'clock in the morning. Denise Diane Rawson, known to everyone as DeDe, lay fast asleep. Her dog, Cookie, lay on the rug in front of the bed. She was sleeping, too. Suddenly a loud noise broke the silence. Cookie lifted her head, but DeDe only shuddered under her blankets. Ten seconds later, another blast followed the first. This time DeDe sat up in bed and reached for her alarm clock. She squinted to read the luminous dial. As her eyes focused, she heard the noise again. It wasn't the alarm clock and it wasn't time to get up.

The door of DeDe's bedroom burst open. Cookie jumped to attention and barked at the intruder.

"DeDe," said an alarmed voice. "What's happening?"

"I don't know, Mom," said DeDe. "It sounds like an invasion from outer space."

Mrs. Rawson turned on the light in DeDe's room and screamed.

"What is it?" gasped DeDe.

Mrs. Rawson giggled nervously. "I forgot about your headgear. It startled me."

DeDe was wearing a device in her mouth that fastened behind her head. The orthodontist said it would make her teeth look better, but now they looked even worse. She was lucky she didn't have to wear it to school. She only put it on at night.

Twice during the seconds she stared at herself in the mirror, the loud noise recurred.

"What is that awful honking?" Mrs. Rawson shuddered. She sat down on DeDe's bed clutching her bathrobe around her. Cookie jumped up on the bed to see what was happening. She wasn't permitted on the bed under usual circumstances, but she knew these were not usual circumstances.

The sound was repeated at regular intervals.

"It could be a code message to a spacecraft," suggested DeDe. The noise did remind her of something, maybe the science-fiction film she had seen a few weeks ago with her father. Somehow she didn't even feel scared. She wondered if she should take off her headgear. She didn't want to frighten a Martian.

"Don't be silly," said her mother. "It sounds like there's a goose in the house."

"A goose? That's even sillier than a Martian," said DeDe. "How could it be a goose?"

"Maybe it's a chicken?"

"Oh, Mom," said DeDe, getting off her bed to look out the window. "Maybe a spaceship has landed."

"Here in Woodside, New Jersey?"

"Why not?" asked DeDe. You could always hope. But there was nothing unusual outside the window.

"We had better look around," said Mrs. Rawson, grabbing her daughter by the hand. She put her other hand on Cookie's collar. "Come," she said to the dog, who would have followed them anyway. "Let's stick together."

It was hard going. Cookie didn't understand about sticking together. She liked to race ahead.

"Do the sounds seem louder in the hallway?" Mrs. Rawson asked.

"I don't know," said DeDe. The sound kept echoing in her ears, even when she didn't actually hear it.

"Maybe we should call the police," said her mother.

"Just because we hear a little noise?" asked DeDe. She imagined armed police surrounding her house. Wouldn't that be something to tell Aldo at school tomorrow!

Cookie growled.

"What is it, Cookie?" Mrs. Rawson asked anxiously.

"It might be something she smells," suggested DeDe.

The dog didn't answer. And the squawking continued. They went from room to room turning on lights and looking around. There was nothing unusual. "We'd better check out the basement," said Mrs. Rawson. She let go of DeDe's hand and took a broom out of the kitchen closet.

"You're not going to sweep the basement at this hour?"

"I may need a weapon," whispered her mother. "We don't know what's down there."

DeDe thought her mother had gone bonkers. The only thing in the basement was the furnace and the Ping-Pong table. When her parents got divorced, her father had packed up all his tools and sold them together with his workbench. "I've had enough of home repairs," he had said as he pasted price tags on the drills and hammers that he had used from time to time.

The Ping-Pong table was covered with dust, its net dropped off the table. DeDe and her father used to play a game together before dinner almost every evening. But it was months since she had picked up one of the little paddles. She didn't even know if there were any balls around anymore.

"There's nothing down here," said DeDe. "At least nothing that doesn't belong here." She noticed her mother's pottery kiln in the corner. It had been so long since her mother had used it that DeDe had even forgotten it was there.

"We can hardly hear the noise down here," said Mrs. Rawson.

"Let's sleep down here, then. We could lie on the Ping-Pong table, and the noise won't wake us."

"I must find out what it is," said Mrs. Rawson. "Not knowing is driving me mad."

They started back up to the kitchen. DeDe and Cookie climbed up together.

"Stop," said Mrs. Rawson. "See? It gets louder the higher you go."

"Maybe there really is a goose like you said."

"There's a goose in the attic. I'm sure of it now," said Mrs. Rawson.

"How could it get in?" asked DeDe. She wasn't so sure.

"I'll get the ladder," said Mrs. Rawson, rushing back down the stairs. She returned dragging the ladder and the broom.

"An angry goose can be dangerous," she told DeDe as she tried to poise the ladder under the trapdoor of the attic. "I'd better get something to put on for protection. Wait here."

"Where would I go?" asked DeDe. But she knew the answer.

Her mother returned wearing leather boots, very fashionable ones with high heels that looked ridiculous with her bathrobe. She also put on a pair of big yellow-and-green gardening gloves. They didn't look so hot with her purple bathrobe, either. "Now, you hand me the broom when I ask for it," said Mrs. Rawson.

The trapdoor was heavy and difficult to lift. Bits of dust began falling down on DeDe and the floor.

"This is making me sneeze," DeDe complained.

"Wait a minute. I'm getting it now," panted Mrs. Rawson. "Quick. Give me the broom."

DeDe handed the broom up to her mother. "I can't see a thing up here," Mrs. Rawson said. "Maybe we should call the fire department. They're supposed to help at times like this."

"There's no fire, Mom," said DeDe, peering into the dark attic. And as soon as she spoke those words, she realized that there was no goose up there, either. She called up to her mother.

"What is it?" asked Mrs. Rawson. "Did the goose fly down? I don't see it anywhere." She clumped down the ladder awkwardly. Her boots had not been designed for this kind of thing.

"The goose isn't a goose," said DeDe.

"You mean it's a chicken?" asked her mother.

"No. Not a goose and not a chicken."

"Then what is it, for heaven's sake?"

"It's the smoke detector. Remember, Dad installed one last year? When the battery runs out, it makes that noise to warn you. Dad explained it to us," said DeDe.

"Some warning," sighed Mrs. Rawson. "It took ten years off my life."

"I can fix it," said DeDe. She pulled the ladder over to where the smoke detector was, and climbed up. It took just a second to remove the dying battery.

"Here's your goose," she said, holding it up.

Her mother's face was smudged with dust, her bathrobe hung open, and her good boots didn't look so good any longer.

"I want something to eat," said Mrs. Rawson, going down to the kitchen. DeDe followed.

"You're not going to start eating at this hour, are you?" she asked.

"Why not?" said Mrs. Rawson. "I must have burned up about a thousand calories on this wild-goose chase." She rinsed her hands at the kitchen sink. Then she opened the door of the refrigerator and pulled out the macaroni and cheese left over from supper.

"Cold macaroni?" DeDe made a face.

Her mother pulled a fat strand of pasta from the dish with her fingers and put it into her mouth. Under her bathrobe, Mrs. Rawson was twenty pounds heavier than she had been before the divorce. It was funny how her father had lost weight and her mother had gained it these past months, DeDe thought. Everyone said that Mr. Rawson had never looked better. DeDe's mother was still a pretty woman, but if she didn't watch out, she would soon be huge.

Cookie sat on the kitchen floor wagging her tail hopefully. She would eat cold macaroni, too, if given half a chance.

"I'm going to sleep," DeDe told her mother. Cookie looked at DeDe with big brown doggy eyes. The dog's loyalty was being tested. The macaroni won, and Cookie stayed in the kitchen.

DeDe went upstairs to bed.

Two

A.D. and B.D.

DeDe had switched off her alarm clock in the middle of the night, so it didn't ring the next morning. She woke up late and raced around the house looking for her sneakers. Mrs. Rawson staggered around the kitchen, half-awake.

"What a night," she said as DeDe tore past her to grab her schoolbooks.

"Where's my lunch?" DeDe called.

"I'll make it now," her mother said.

"I'm late," DeDe shrieked.

"Take it easy," Mrs. Rawson called back as she spread some mustard on a slice of bread. "Take Cookie for a quick walk and I'll drive you to school. I don't have to be at the store until eleven today."

Mrs. Rawson had a job in a department store. Among the changes that the divorce had brought about was her mother's new schedule. Lots of mothers worked, Dede knew. But Mrs. Rawson worked different hours all the time. Her schedule changed from day to day and from week to week. It was because she was new at the store. But soon she would have regular hours and make more money. DeDe sighed. She had never thought about money before her parents' divorce. Her father had a good job, and there had always been enough money for everything. He still had a good job, but now he had to support two households on the same salary.

When DeDe came back into the house with Cookie, her mother was just putting aluminum foil around the sandwich. "Do you have change for milk?" she asked.

DeDe nodded as she gulped down a glass of orange juice. "Let's get going," she said. "It's late."

Mrs. Rawson put her trench coat over her bathrobe. She was still wearing her bedroom slippers, but it wouldn't matter inside the car. DeDe slid in next to her mother. She could hear Cookie barking her good-byes from the house.

Mrs. Rawson turned the key in the ignition. There was a sputter and then nothing. "I'd better wait so I don't flood the motor," Mrs. Rawson said.

"I'll be late," DeDe whined.

"It only takes a few minutes in the car," said her mother, turning the key again. Nothing happened.

"She's dead," said Mrs. Rawson. "She won't start."

"Not again," wailed DeDe. The car conked out whenever they were in a rush. "How come the car never did this when Dad was here?" DeDe demanded.

"It's a year older now," Mrs. Rawson said, sighing. "We all are. You'd better walk to school. I'll call the garage."

"I could have made it to school before. Now I'm really late," DeDe fumed.

"Come inside and I'll write a note to your teacher explaining everything."

"Don't explain *everything*," said DeDe. She didn't want her mother telling the teacher about the goose in the attic. "Just say the car broke down."

Cookie was delighted to see DeDe and her mother again so soon. Mrs. Rawson wrote a short note and said good-bye. Then she began to dial the garage. DeDe noticed that her mother didn't even have to check the number in the telephone book. She knew the number by heart.

DeDe trudged off to school in disgust. Something always seemed to be going wrong these days. The dishwasher had been broken for two months now, and her mother wasn't even going to get it fixed. "Two people don't make that many dirty dishes," she said, shrugging her shoulders. But nobody said they had to use it every day. They could wait until it was full. It had been nice not doing dishes. Now they had to be done every day or else!

The worst thing of all had been one day when DeDe had come home from school with Aldo Sossi, her best friend, and damp shirts, socks, skirts, and jeans were draped over every piece of furniture.

"The dryer's broken," her mother explained. "Be thankful everything is clean. Next week the washing machine may go."

Aldo acted like it was perfectly normal to walk into a house and see wet laundry everywhere. But DeDe had never been more embarrassed, especially when Aldo saw her underpants hanging from the mantle of the fireplace.

Aldo politely turned his back, only to find himself staring right at two of Mrs. Rawson's bras.

"Mom. This is disgusting," DeDe screamed.

"Shouting won't help the clothes dry," her mother admonished.

"How come things always break in this house? They don't at Aldo's," DeDe yelled. Everything in Aldo's life seemed fine to her. He had two older sisters and two cats and two parents who lived together. No fights, no di-

vorces, no problems, and no broken appliances.

"Our dryer broke once, too," Aldo said. "My sister Elaine was angry because she wanted to wear her new jeans to a party. So we put them in the oven."

"You cooked them?" asked DeDe.

Aldo nodded. "It was my father's idea. It worked, too."

"That was very resourceful," said Mrs. Rawson. She began to gather up the damp clothing with Aldo helping her. DeDe rushed across the room and grabbed her underpants. If anyone was going to put them in the oven, she didn't want it to be Aldo.

"After the dryer broke, my father took some books out of the library about how to fix things. My mother took a plumbing course in Adult Ed."

DeDe could imagine Mrs. Sossi armed with a plunger, marching into the house. At least their toilet was still working, she thought as at last she arrived at school. She was tired out from rushing and from the one-sided fight she had been having with her mother along the way. DeDe showed her note to the school secretary and took it upstairs to her class-room.

As she slid into her seat, DeDe caught Al-do's eye. At lunchtime she would tell him *some* of the reasons she was late to school.

The fifth-graders were in the middle of math. DeDe took out her workbook and yawned. She hated to feel tired when she had just woken up. It was all because of the wild-goose chase. This was going to be a very long day.

After math there was social studies. Mrs. Sussman turned off the lights to show a film-strip about life in France. DeDe dug her fin-gernails into her palms to keep herself awake. Her eyes kept wanting to close. Lunch didn't rouse DeDe either. The afternoon seemed to pass even slower than the morning.

There was a clock in the back of the room, and from time to time, DeDe turned her head to see how much longer it was till the bell rang.

"Do you have an appointment some-where?" Mrs. Sussman asked when she caught

DeDe sneaking a look for the third time in a half-hour.

DeDe blushed and turned around in her seat. Mrs. Sussman was teaching a lesson about the calendar. "Why are some years B.C. and others A.D.?" she asked. She wrote the letters on the board.

DeDe yawned again. It was funny to see the letters *A B C D* on the blackboard, as if she were just learning the alphabet.

She wrote the letters A.D. on her paper.

"I'm glad to see that DeDe is taking notes," said Mrs. Sussman. "Traci, why isn't your notebook open?"

DeDe leaned closer over her paper. She didn't want anyone to see what she had written.

A.D. = After Divorce, B.D. = Before Divorce. That was another way to measure time, she thought. She wished she had never entered A.D.

Three

An Odd Weekend

The way her parents had arranged things after their divorce, whenever Friday fell on an odd number, DeDe spent the weekend with her father. Not only did Mr. Rawson get custody of DeDe on those odd weekends, he had custody of Cookie, too. Mrs. Rawson had seen to that.

The Friday following the Tuesday morning wild-goose chase was an odd one. When school was over, DeDe packed her overnight bag, and her mother drove into New York City where Mr. Rawson had an apartment.

"Have a good time," Mrs. Rawson called as DeDe and Cookie jumped out of the car.

Cookie barked happily. She enjoyed car rides, but she liked city smells even better.

Mrs. Rawson didn't turn off the motor. With a new starter, it was running again, but probably she didn't want to press her luck.

"See you Sunday," she called as DeDe and Cookie walked up to Mr. Rawson's building.

George, the doorman, greeted DeDe and Cookie. DeDe waved good-bye and watched the old car weave into the early-evening traffic before she turned to George.

"Your father isn't home yet," he told her. "I can get the super to let you into the apart-ment with his passkey, or you can sit in the lobby and wait."

"I think I'll take Cookie for a walk," said DeDe. She left her bag with George.

There were many other dogs taking walks, and Cookie wanted to greet them all. She also seemed to want to check that her favorite lamp post and fire hydrant were still there.

Mr. Rawson's apartment was on Riverside Drive. His building faced the Hudson River, and you could look across and see New Jersey. DeDe thought of her mother driving back to an empty house.

Cookie pulled hard, and DeDe turned her head. This time it was a stray cat that had caught Cookie's attention.

A cold wind blew off the river, and after a few minutes of walking, DeDe decided to go into the building to wait. There was a big, overstuffed couch in the lobby that she liked to sit on. The couch faced the door, and she would see her father the moment he entered the building.

It was interesting to watch the people coming home from work. She saw several women the same age as her mother who were all dressed in elegant clothes and wore lots of makeup. DeDe wondered how her mother would look in clothing like that. Maybe if she'd worn clothes like that, her husband wouldn't have left.

DeDe thought back to the time B.D., almost a year ago, when her parents had announced that they were getting divorced. DeDe knew about divorce from TV and the movies, but she hadn't realized that it could happen to someone in Woodside, New Jersey. Now she knew it could.

A little girl ran into the lobby, followed by her mother and father, who were each holding the hand of a very little boy. "Oooops-a-daisy," said the father as he and his wife raised their arms and made the boy's feet swing off the ground. DeDe wondered what they were going to have for dinner and if they would all sit together and watch television afterward.

"Nice doggie," said the little boy. He let go of his parents' hands and ran to Cookie.

Cookie wagged her tail in pleasure.

"Come, Bradley," called the boy's mother as the elevator door opened. The family disappeared inside, and DeDe and Cookie sat watching. And still Mr. Rawson did not come.

"Some days those subways take longer than walking," George said as DeDe shifted anxiously on the couch. Suppose her father had forgotten that she was coming?

24

DeDe could see that it was getting darker outside. Suddenly Cookie pulled on her leash and let out a bark of greeting.

"Hi ya, sweetheart," her father's voice called out. Mr. Rawson dropped his briefcase and threw his arms around his daughter. DeDe felt the scratchiness of his mustache on her cheek. Cookie ran in circles around them, and the leash got tangled with their legs.

"Sorry I'm late," Mr. Rawson apologized as he freed them from the leash. "Are you hungry?"

"You bet," said DeDe. She felt good now that she and her father were together again. She wondered where they would go to eat. Her father never cooked. He always took her to a restaurant, and she could order anything she wanted.

"Great. Let's just drop our things in the apartment. Let me see your teeth," he said as they rode up to the fifteenth floor in the elevator. "I'm paying enough for them."

DeDe grinned so that her father could get a good look at her malocclusion.

"I'm the only divorced kid in my class," she

told her father. "But four other kids have braces and more are going to be getting them."

"There may well be more divorces, too," said her father. "You got these teeth from your mother. My teeth knew how they were supposed to grow. And I want you to have perfect teeth, too."

DeDe didn't think her mother's teeth looked so bad. But her father had insisted that she get braces and Dr. Curry, their dentist, had agreed. "Well-aligned teeth get fewer cavities," he had told them last spring.

Mr. Rawson opened the door to his apartment. It was so tiny that it made DeDe think of playing house. Everything was fresh and new, and DeDe had helped pick the sofa bed she slept on. But by Sunday she always felt as if things were a bit cramped. And Cookie was always knocking things over. She couldn't help it in such close quarters. The walls were so thin, you could hear if someone was watching the television next door. And once, when DeDe was brushing her teeth in the bathroom, she heard someone else brushing theirs.

"Happy birthday, Dad," said DeDe, removing a small, wrapped package from her bag. She watched anxiously as her father opened it. This was the first year DeDe's mother had not gone shopping with her for her father's gift. Her mother's birthday was a month later, and in years past, her father had always helped her choose and pay for a gift for her mother. A.D. had changed all that.

Mr. Rawson tore off the wrapping paper. Underneath was a small notebook covered with marbleized paper, which DeDe had made at school. "It's for an address book," said DeDe helpfully. "You know so many new people nowadays."

"It's lovely," said Mr. Rawson. "It's also a bit sticky."

"I guess the glue didn't finish drying," said DeDe. "I was in a hurry to bring it."

"Sure," said Mr. Rawson, washing his hands. "Look over here," he said. "This time I didn't forget."

On the kitchen table were cans of dog food. Two weeks ago, her father had forgotten to buy dog food. Cookie's supper had been a quarter of a pound of liver paté that Mr. Rawson had found inside his refrigerator. Cookie had happily gobbled this unexpected treat, but later she had gotten sick and thrown up on Mr. Rawson's new rug.

DeDe served out the dog food to Cookie. The can said that it contained all the vitamins and minerals that a dog needed to be happy and healthy. The paté had probably lacked those things.

"Too bad you can't come with us, Cookie," said Mr. Rawson as he and DeDe prepared to leave the apartment.

DeDe giggled. "Who ever heard of a dog eating in a restaurant?" she said.

The restaurant was nearby. As they walked, they caught up on each other's news. Mr. Rawson had joined a health club where he went two evenings a week to run around the track and swim in the pool. He patted his stomach. "I'm getting into great shape."

DeDe told her father about life in Woodside. They laughed about the smoke detector that had scared Mrs. Rawson half to death. Then DeDe wondered if she was being disloyal to her mother, and so she changed the subject. "I got 105 on my math test this week," she reported proudly. It was her best subject at school.

"How can you get 105?" asked her father. "When I went to school, you couldn't do better than 100."

"There were two extra-credit problems, and I got one right," DeDe explained.

Mr. Rawson nodded. "I guess with inflation these days, you need to get more than one hundred," he said.

At the restaurant, DeDe didn't need to read the menu. She knew what she wanted—a broiled lobster. She smiled at her father as the waiter tied a plastic bib around her neck. Since her father had moved to New York, she must have eaten at least a dozen lobsters. B.D. she had never even tasted one.

"Janice and I have eaten here a few times," Mr. Rawson said. "They cook the fish perfectly here."

DeDe nodded as she extracted meat from a lobster claw. Her father liked perfection. He wanted his apartment to be perfect. His meals

had to be perfect. Even DeDe's teeth had to be perfect. She thought about the sticky little notebook. It wasn't perfect. She wondered if he would use it.

DeDe also thought about her father's friend Janice. DeDe had met her a few times. Janice was pretty and friendly, but she owned a fur jacket. DeDe didn't approve of fur coats, and she wasn't sure if she approved of Janice, either.

"Are you going to marry Janice?" DeDe asked her father.

"No," he answered quickly. "I enjoy her company. But I'm looking for the perfect woman, and I won't marry again until I find her."

"Was Mom perfect when you married her?" DeDe asked.

This time Mr. Rawson didn't answer so quickly. "She seemed perfect to me."

"Did she change?" asked DeDe.

"I guess we both changed. I don't love your mother, and I can't live with her anymore. She feels the same about me."

"What about me?" asked DeDe. "I'm not

perfect. Is that why you don't want to live with me?"

"But you are perfect," her father said, leaning over and putting his arm around her. "To your mother and me, you will always be perfect. But since you can't live in two places at once, it seemed better for you to stay in Woodside."

"What about my teeth?" asked DeDe. "They're not perfect."

"No. But it is possible to correct them. Don't forget, I loved you before you had any teeth."

DeDe thought she understood. But when they were finishing their meal, her father said, "It's just possible that we won't be able to spend some of our weekends together as planned."

"What do you mean?" DeDe asked.

"I've got to make a trip to California next week," her father said. "I'll be back in time for your next visit, but after that, I'm not sure. You know that my company is expanding. I'm going to be very busy for a while." He put down his fork and covered her hand with his. "I'll miss you very much," he said.

"Couldn't I go to California to see you?" asked DeDe.

Mr. Rawson shook his head. "It's too expensive to fly you back and forth just for a weekend. Besides, I'll be too busy to entertain you."

DeDe swallowed a mouthful of dessert. It didn't taste as good as it had a moment before.

"Come," said DeDe's father as they stood up to leave the restaurant. "Don't let what might happen in a few weeks spoil your weekend now."

DeDe tried to smile, but she felt her eyes filling with tears. How could you miss someone when you were standing right next to him? she wondered. But that's the way she felt now. She was already missing her father.

Four

The Vegetable Club

At school on Monday, Aldo mentioned that his mother was starting a vegetable club.

"What's that?" DeDe asked. She imagined celery and cucumbers holding a meeting.

"It's a way to save money," Aldo explained. "People get together and buy vegetables in bulk in order to get a better price."

"Could my mother join?" asked DeDe. "She's always saying we should save money."

"Sure," said Aldo. "I'll tell my mother."

DeDe didn't actually know if her mother would be interested, but she thought it was worth a try. Her father had joined a club, and he seemed very happy. It would be good for her mother to join something, too, but there was no health club or singles club in Woodside. There was only the Girl Scouts and Little League Baseball, neither of which were for a woman her mother's age. There was also Weight Watchers. Her mother could qualify for that group. But DeDe didn't want her mother meeting and dating fat men.

That evening, when Mrs. Rawson came home from work, DeDe greeted her with the news. "Aldo's mother is starting a club, and I told Aldo to tell her that you would like to join."

"Maybe I wouldn't like to join," said Mrs. Rawson. "What sort of a club is it?"

"A vegetable club."

"What's that? A club for tomato- and asparagus-lovers?"

DeDe repeated what Aldo had told her.

"Oh, Dede," said Mrs. Rawson, taking off

her high heels and rubbing her feet. "We don't eat enough vegetables for that club."

"Wait. There's more than just vegetables," said DeDe eagerly. "There's fruit, too."

"I guess it's a good idea for big families, but there are just the two of us," said Mrs. Rawson. "You'll have to tell Mrs. Sossi that I'm not interested."

"But, Mom," DeDe protested, "just last week you were complaining about how expensive everything is in the supermarket."

"That's true," her mother admitted. "But—"

"And joining a club is a good way to meet new people. That's very important for a divorced woman."

"New people, yes," agreed Mrs. Rawson, "but I'm not interested in getting to know a handsome and dashing stalk of celery or a successful and brilliant young broccoli."

Mrs. Rawson headed toward the kitchen. DeDe followed her.

"Mrs. Sossi is going to call tonight. At least talk to her," she begged.

Dinner was a tuna fish-and-noodle casserole, and they had sliced tomatoes with it.

When her mother had seen the price of the tomatoes, she had said, "They probably have diamonds inside." Of course there was only tomato inside the tomato. So maybe Mrs. Sossi would be able to convince her mother to join the vegetable club after all.

The telephone rang as they were washing the dishes, and DeDe could guess that it was Aldo's mother. Although she herself didn't like most vegetables, DeDe silently promised to eat more of them if her mother joined the club.

When Mrs. Rawson hung up the phone, she told DeDe that she had joined. "I agreed to take a half-membership on a trial basis." There were already a dozen families in the food co-op, but one was a young couple with a baby, and they didn't need as much as families with older children. They wanted to split their membership, and that's where the Rawsons came in. They would get a half-share of the fruits and vegetables every two weeks.

"Great!" shouted DeDe. Cookie caught her enthusiasm and began to run around barking.

"Hey, Cookie," Mrs. Rawson called, "you don't even eat vegetables!"

Cookie *really* barked the day the first load of vegetables was delivered to the house. It was a Wednesday, the one day her mother never worked. DeDe came home from school and found her mother in the kitchen counting out piles of carrots and beets and cabbages and squash.

"Yikes!" gasped DeDe. "I didn't know it would be so much." If she stayed home from school for the next two weeks and did nothing but eat vegetables, they probably still wouldn't use them up.

Mrs. Rawson began to laugh. "Relax," she said. "It isn't all for us. At five o'clock the other members will be coming to pick up their shares. But I've been waiting for you. I sure need help, and Cookie doesn't know a bean from a beet."

DeDe peeled off her jacket and started counting heads of cabbage. There were twenty-four, which meant that each family got two, except for the Rawsons and the Collinses, who would each get one. That was ac-

tually one more than DeDe wanted since she didn't like cabbage.

There were thirty-six bags of carrots; twenty-four bunches of beets; loads of squash, tomatoes, and mushrooms; and some funny, long things with little round knobs on them.

"Those are brussels sprouts," said Mrs. Rawson. "Don't they look good?"

DeDe wondered what brussels sprouts tasted like and if her mother had a pot big enough to put those long things in.

At last everything was divided. Mrs. Rawson took her share into the kitchen and started to put things away. "Don't these have wonderful shapes?" she asked, admiring the butternut and golden nugget squash. She took an old marker and drew faces on several of them. Then she arranged them on the counter and stepped back, admiring her handiwork.

The door bell rang. Cookie went bounding over the vegetable hurdles, and DeDe followed to open the door. It was the first co-op member coming to pick up her share. DeDe helped the woman load her food into the car. She came in for a moment and gave

Mrs. Rawson a check and then drove off into the dark. If everyone comes and goes that quickly, how could her mother make new friends?

Each arrival was the same. In and out, with DeDe helping to load the cars. Money changed hands, but very few words were spoken. This wasn't the way DeDe had thought the club would be at all. She thought people would come inside and visit with her mother. Maybe they would trade recipes. At least they would exchange phone numbers and plan to get together sometime. But even Mr. Sossi, who came with Aldo's sister, Karen, stayed only long enough to pick up their share and take the money Mrs. Rawson had collected from everyone.

When all the boxes and bags were gone, DeDe sat down on the sofa, exhausted.

Mrs. Rawson was pulling pots out of the cupboard.

"We're going to have ratatouille! I haven't made that in years."

"Rat-tat-too-ee! Phooey!" DeDe moaned. What had she gotten them into?

Five

The Birthday Surprise

First it had been her father's birthday, and now it was her mother's. DeDe didn't know how she could make her mother happy. Mrs. Rawson had a job with long hours and low pay, a car that only ran sometimes, a house in need of repairs, and a daughter without enough money to get her anything special. What could DeDe buy for $2.45? Not much.

Aldo suggested that DeDe make her mother something.

"I just started a birdhouse in shop," DeDe told him, "but it won't be ready for ages."

"You could draw a picture of it and give that to her. Tell her she'll get the real thing when it's finished," said Aldo.

"Big thrill," said DeDe. "A picture of a birdhouse for your birthday. At least she won't have to worry about paying heating bills for it."

"Last year for my parents' fifteenth wedding anniversary, Elaine and Karen and I made our own cards, and we wrapped up a bar of Ivory soap."

"Soap?" said DeDe. "That's as bad as a picture of a birdhouse."

"It was a joke. You're supposed to give a gift made out of ivory for a fifteenth anniversary."

If it was a joke, DeDe didn't think it was very funny. She asked Traci, the girl who sat next to her in class, if she had any ideas about a birthday present for her mother.

"I always write a birthday poem," said Traci. "I've been doing it since second grade. My mom thinks it's great, and it doesn't cost anything."

43

"I couldn't do that," sighed DeDe.

"I'll write one for you," offered Traci.

"Would you really?" asked DeDe.

"You'll have to pay me," said Traci.

"How much?"

Traci thought a moment. "Fifty cents," she said.

DeDe considered the offer. "I'll have to see it first," she said.

"Then you have to give me a kill fee," said Traci.

"What's that?"

"If I write something and you don't like it, I should get paid at least a dime for my effort. My father is a writer, so I know all about things like that," Traci explained.

There wasn't anything you could buy for a dime, anyway, so DeDe agreed.

"How old is your mother going to be?" Traci asked.

"Thirty-two."

"Good. Just like mine," said Traci, nodding her head with approval. Thirty was a hard year. The only rhyme I could make was *dirty.* I'll have the poem for you by tomorrow," she promised.

The next day Traci slid a piece of paper onto DeDe's desk during social studies.

For my mom, who I love very much
Or else I would not make a card as such.
This is your birthday
So good for you
You now have reached thirty-two.
As I write to you, I try to express
The love for you that I possess
Even though my room is a mess.
All in all, I'd like to say
You're a great mom, so stay that way.
I love you, Mom!

DeDe read it through twice. "How did you know my room was messy?" she whispered. Traci had never come to her house.

"All kids have messy rooms," Traci whispered back.

"DeDe? Are you doing your map?" called Mrs. Sussman.

"Yes," answered DeDe, although she wasn't.

"Good," said the teacher.

DeDe looked down at the poem. She decided that her mother would be pleased with

it. At lunchtime, she gave Traci two quarters. "Thanks a lot," she told her. "I'll copy
it over in my own handwriting."

"I'm sure she'll like it," said Traci. "My
mother loved it."

"Did you show it to her?" asked DeDe.

"It's the same one that I gave her for her
birthday."

"The same one?"

Traci nodded, beaming at the two coins in
her hand. "These are the first royalties I ever
earned from my writing," she said. "Maybe I
should advertise. I could sell poems for
birthdays and Christmas and Mother's Day
and things like that."

DeDe didn't want to give her mother a
secondhand poem. "Here," she said, handing the poem back to Traci. "I want my
money back."

"Then you still owe me a dime."

They exchanged coins and DeDe was back
where she had started, without her dime or
a gift for her mother.

On the way home from school, she said to
Aldo. "I wish I was good in the kitchen like

your sister Karen. Then I could bake a cake for my mom."

"Let's ask Karen," suggested Aldo. "I bet she'd make one for you."

Aldo's sister loved to bake. "You'll have to pay for the ingredients," she told DeDe. "But I'll make anything you want."

"I only have $2.35," DeDe explained. "Will that be enough?"

Karen began figuring out the price of eggs and butter and flour on a piece of paper. "I won't make anything using chocolate," she said. She figured some more. "Maybe you have some of the ingredients in your house already."

"What's the cheapest cake you can make?" asked DeDe.

Karen considered for a moment. "I've got a great recipe for carrot cake," she said.

DeDe looked doubtful.

"It's delicious!" said Aldo. "We get so many carrots from the vegetable club that Karen makes that cake to use them up."

DeDe remembered that there were at least three bags of carrots in the refrigerator at home that very moment, and a new delivery was due next week.

"Will the cake have frosting on it?" she asked.

"Make that peppermint frosting," Aldo suggested.

Karen shook her head. "It's too much like toothpaste. I'll make a cream-cheese frosting. Your mother will love it," she promised DeDe. "And so will you."

DeDe was to deliver a bag of carrots and her $2.35 to Karen the next afternoon, and Karen would deliver the finished cake to DeDe's house by four-thirty on Monday.

Mrs. Rawson didn't get home from work on Monday till after five o'clock so when Aldo and Karen arrived carrying the cake, there was plenty of time for DeDe to admire it. Karen had even managed to write out "For Mom," using chocolate bits. "We had a bag of them, so I threw these in as a bonus," she said.

"Imagine making a cake out of a bag of carrots," said DeDe. "Do you have any good recipes for brussels sprouts?"

"I don't think you can make a cake out of

Brussels sprouts," said Karen. "But you'll have to try my chocolate zucchini cake sometime."

"I wish I could pay you," said DeDe.

"That's okay," said Karen. "If I only make things for my family to eat, we'll all get fat."

DeDe cleared the kitchen table and put the cake on a platter in the center. "I won't tell my mother it's here," she said. "It will be a surprise."

Karen and Aldo decided to wait for Mrs. Rawson.

The three of them went up to DeDe's room. Karen stopped to admire the planters hanging in the windows. "Where did you buy them?" she asked.

"My mother made them," said DeDe proudly. The planters were in the shape of heads. Some were women and some were men. The green leaves growing out of them looked like hair. Karen's favorite was a woman who had long, dangling earrings and a spider plant growing out of her head.

"Come on, I'll show you some others," said DeDe. She took Karen and Aldo around the house, pointing out all the planters and vases and bowls that her mother had made.

"My mother used to make a lot of stuff and sell it at craft fairs. But since she got divorced, she doesn't have much time."

Cookie went around with them for a while, but she soon got bored. "Your dog doesn't appreciate art," said Karen when Cookie didn't bother to follow them into DeDe's mother's bedroom.

DeDe heard the front door bang shut.

"Hi, Mom," shouted DeDe. She gestured for Aldo and Karen to hide behind the door as she walked out into the hallway to greet her mother.

"How was your day?" she asked.

"Okay," sighed Mrs. Rawson, slipping off her heels and putting on her loafers. "Another day, another dollar."

Mrs. Rawson sank down onto the living room sofa.

"Aren't you going into the kitchen?" hinted DeDe.

"Are you hungry?" asked her mother. "You can go preheat the oven to 350 degrees, if you want to speed things up."

"But aren't you going into the kitchen?" DeDe urged.

"Not yet," said Mrs. Rawson. "It's been a long day."

DeDe waited impatiently for a minute or so. "Couldn't you start supper now?" she asked.

"For heaven's sake," complained Mrs. Rawson. "Let me catch my breath."

Cookie came into the living room and put her head into Mrs. Rawson's lap.

"Why, Cookie," said DeDe's mother, "you didn't even bother to greet me. I suppose you're hungry, too." She patted the dog. "Well, I'm not feeding you. That's DeDe's job."

DeDe didn't want to go into the kitchen to open a can of dog food. She wanted her mother to go in there first and find the cake.

Finally Mrs. Rawson got up. She turned on the light in the kitchen.

DeDe ran up behind her mother and shouted, "Surprise. Happy Birthday!"

Hearing her shout, Aldo and Karen ran out of the bedroom.

"Happy birthday, Mrs. Rawson!" they chimed in.

"Do you like it?" asked Karen.

Mrs. Rawson stood blocking the entrance to the kitchen. DeDe pushed past her mother. There was a platter and some crumbs on the kitchen table. DeDe saw two of the little chocolate bits. But the cake itself was gone.

"What happened?" she shrieked.

"What happened?" echoed her mother.

Cookie jumped up on the table and licked up the crumbs that she had missed.

"Oh, Mom," DeDe cried out. "Karen made a birthday cake and Cookie ate it."

"It was a carrot cake with cream-cheese frosting," said Karen. "It had six carrots in it."

"Cookie," said Aldo to the dog, who was happily wagging her tail. "You're going to be able to see in the dark now that you ate so many carrots."

"She'll be a Seeing Eye dog," said DeDe. How could she have been so stupid? Cookie was notorious for eating everything in sight.

"Well, at least she didn't make a mess," said Mrs. Rawson. "There's barely a crumb left."

"I could make another cake," offered Karen. "But I won't be able to deliver it before tomorrow."

"Oh, Mom," said DeDe, hugging her mother. "I wanted so much to surprise you."

"But I am surprised!" Mrs. Rawson insisted, hugging DeDe to her.

Karen took another bag of carrots out of the refrigerator before she and Aldo left. "I'll see you tomorrow," she promised.

"Look at it this way," consoled Mrs. Rawson. "Now we only have to finish up one bag of carrots before the next delivery."

"Oh, Cookie, you take the cake," DeDe sighed as she helped her mother clean up the few remaining crumbs.

Six

Stuffed Cabbage

eDe opened the refrigerator to get an apple, and two cabbages rolled out. On every shelf in the refrigerator there were bags of carrots, bunches of beets, radishes, cucumbers, squash, celery, tomatoes, mushrooms, artichokes, brussels sprouts, and cauliflower.

"I wish Cookie would eat them," DeDe said as she picked up the cabbages from the floor. Cookie, who would normally eat anything that wasn't nailed down, wanted no part of the vegetables, aside from the carrot cake, that is. DeDe wanted no part of them, either. Even when her mother prepared dishes with fancy sauces and fancy names, DeDe hated them. They had had beans vinaigrette, cauliflower au gratin, and brussels sprouts polonaise. It was too much to ask a normal American girl to eat so many foreign vegetables. But the vegetable club had been her idea, so she couldn't complain. Her mother hadn't made a single new friend, but she had begun packing large salads to take to work for her lunch. Every vegetable eaten was a triumph!

"Why don't you give a party and cook up all these things," DeDe suggested. The idea had just popped into her head.

"I'd do almost anything to be able to find the eggs again," sighed Mrs. Rawson. "But I'm not so sure about a party. It's hard to entertain when you're a single woman. Some couples act as if divorce might be catching, like chicken pox."

"You could make stuffed cabbage," said DeDe. She knew she had her mother there.

Two weeks ago Mrs. Rawson had made stuffed cabbage. DeDe had eaten one of the rolled cabbage leaves filled with chopped meat and rice and said, "Why can't we just have plain meatballs without wrapping them in cabbage?"

"How would we use up the cabbage, then?" asked her mother. There was no question about it. Their whole life now revolved around using up the vegetables.

"A dinner party might be nice," said Mrs. Rawson. "I haven't seen anyone in months." She began making a list of guests.

DeDe grinned as she watched her. It would even be worth eating leftover stuffed cabbage if her mother had a party. Mrs. Rawson's life didn't seem very exciting to DeDe. Her biggest thrill came when the car started in the morning.

Mrs. Rawson made a few calls that evening. Some of the old friends she called were going to be busy on Saturday evening. But three couples promised to come—all friends from the B.D. days.

"I'll make stuffed cabbage and beet salad

and a pot of vegetable soup," DeDe's mother planned aloud.

Every evening for the rest of the week, as DeDe sat doing her homework or watching television, her mother happily chopped vegetables in the kitchen. Soon, the refrigerator was filled with pots of cooked vegetables, boiled, stuffed, steamed, and pureed.

That weekend Friday fell on an even number, so DeDe was staying home. She helped her mother clean on Saturday. They put more energy into the vacuuming and dusting than they had for ages. DeDe even got the bottle of window cleaner and did the downstairs windows, though she knew that when the guests arrived, it would be too dark for anyone to notice.

As she worked, she couldn't help noticing that there was a crack in the living room ceiling, and the wallpaper in the hall had begun to peel. It was a long way from her father's perfect apartment. But new wallpaper, paint, and plaster all cost a lot of money. And even in its rundown condition, she still loved her house.

At four-thirty that afternoon, while Mrs. Rawson was out buying candles, the telephone rang. DeDe answered it. Ann Arnold was on the line to say that Harold had come down with the flu and that they wouldn't be able to come that evening. "I'll tell my mother," said DeDe. She was so concerned that her mother would be upset that she forgot to say she hoped Harold would feel better soon. It was very important that this evening go well. After all, it was DeDe who had pushed her mother to give the party in the first place.

Mrs. Rawson was disappointed. But she just rearranged the plates on the table and put the candles in the candlesticks. Then she went to take a shower.

The telephone rang again, and DeDe went to answer it. It was Louise Crosby. She told DeDe that their car had broken down on the Jersey Turnpike and had to be towed away. "We hope it will be fixed by Monday morning. But we have no way of getting out of here tonight."

When DeDe told her, Mrs. Rawson said,

"At least we're not the only ones with car trouble." She sighed and added, "I hope the Martins are very hungry."

"Isn't there anyone else you could call?" asked DeDe. Why had she talked her mother into giving this dinner party, anyhow?

Mrs. Rawson got out her address book. "I hate to call someone on such short notice," she said.

"I wouldn't mind if someone called me now to do something special tonight," said DeDe.

"That's the difference between being eleven and being thirty-two," said Mrs. Rawson. But she continued turning pages in her address book.

There was no one home at Mrs. Rawson's friend Arline's house. The line was busy when she called Carla and George Freeman's house. Then, when she tried again, there was no answer.

"Looks like we're going to be eating stuffed cabbage for weeks," said Mrs. Rawson.

DeDe didn't answer.

The Martins were expected at seven o'clock. The vegetable soup and the stuffed cabbage were simmering on the stove. With the lights dimmed and the cooking aromas filling the house, it had a warm, cozy feeling.

"The Martins are really nice people," said DeDe, trying to make her mother feel better about the evening ahead. "I remember when we went on a picnic with them once when I was little."

Mrs. Rawson nodded. The picnic was another B.D. event. Perhaps it would have been better not to have mentioned it.

"I wonder why they're so late?" Mrs. Rawson said when seven-thirty came and went without a sign of the Martins.

She went to the kitchen to adjust the flames under her pots. "Maybe they thought I said eight o'clock."

The Martins did not arrive at eight o'clock, either.

At ten after eight, Mrs. Rawson went to the telephone. "If they aren't home, it means they're on their way," she said as she dialed.

The Martins were not home, but if they were on their way to the Rawson's, they didn't arrive at eight-thirty or nine o'clock, either.

"Maybe they think your party is next week," suggested DeDe. She could feel the tension in the house. Even Cookie sat quietly in a corner.

Mrs. Rawson went upstairs and changed into her robe. DeDe could see that her eyes were red. She looked the way she often had during the early days of the divorce. It's not my fault, DeDe told herself. But she couldn't help thinking that it was. She should never have suggested the party.

DeDe turned on the television to distract herself.

"Did you do all your homework?" her mother snapped.

Ordinarily, her mother would never have bothered DeDe about homework on a Saturday night.

"Almost," said DeDe.

"Well, turn off the TV until it's all done," she said. She began clearing the table and putting away the unused dishes.

DeDe turned off the television. She sat feeling sorry for herself and sorry for her mother, too. She wished she was with her father. On a Saturday night they would probably be at a movie or the Ice Capades or something. Not just sitting around.

"What homework do you have left?" asked Mrs. Rawson.

"It's social studies," said DeDe. Everyone was given the name of a famous person in French history and instead of just handing in reports we have to act out the whole thing in class."

"Who did you get?" asked her mother.

"Marie Antoinette."

"She shouldn't be hard to do," said Mrs. Rawson.

"It's not so easy to get up in front of the whole class," said DeDe. "I don't know what to do."

Suddenly Mrs. Rawson's expression softened, and she actually smiled. "What if we made a papier-mâché head for you to hold up? You know Marie Antoinette had her head chopped off during the French Revolution. You could hold up the head and say this is what happened to her."

DeDe couldn't help laughing.

Mrs. Rawson, moving much more energetically than she had a minute before, cleared off the rest of the table. She covered it with old newspapers and got a bowl of water. Cookie trotted over to the table to watch as DeDe and her mother made a flour-and-water paste and cut newspapers into strips. DeDe felt that she would always be grateful to Mrs. Sussman. Her teacher would never know how she had saved the rest of the evening. DeDe's mother had gone to art school before she got married, and she was good at all kinds of crafts. There was nothing she enjoyed more.

By the time DeDe went to bed that night, she had a papier-mâché head to show off to her class at school.

DeDe and her mother had also made a very important discovery. Cookie loved stuffed cabbage.

Seven

The Class Play

Twice a month, a play was presented at school assembly. The teachers drew lots, and Mrs. Sussman got the first week in November. "It's too late for Halloween and too early for Thanksgiving," she told the class.

"Then what will we do?" asked Traci.

"We'll build a show around our social studies reports," the teacher said.

Aldo grinned at DeDe. They had both been very happy about the way their reports had

66

turned out. Aldo had been assigned Joan of Arc, and even though he was a boy, he had done such a good job that no one had laughed at him. DeDe's papier-mâché head had caused a sensation. Playing Marie Antoinette had to be better than last year when she'd been a maple tree in a fourth-grade ecology play.

Assemblies were always on Fridays, and the date of the play fell on the Friday of an odd weekend. Many of the children in DeDe's class had said their parents would be coming.

"Do you think Dad would come?" DeDe asked her mother. "Then I could go back to the city with him."

Mrs. Rawson wasn't sure. "You can ask him," she said. "But don't be disappointed if he can't make it. You know how much traveling he's doing these days."

DeDe phoned right after supper. As the telephone rang, she thought of how her mother must have felt when she was inviting people to dinner. She remembered the two couples who didn't show up, and the Martins, who did, although they were a week late.

Don't say no. Don't say no, she pleaded silently.

"Hello, this is Henry Rawson," said DeDe's father's voice. "I am not at home at the moment, but I will return your call as soon as possible. At the signal, please leave your name, phone number, and a brief message. You will have twenty seconds." There was a pause and then a tone. DeDe couldn't say a word. She was so busy wondering how long twenty seconds was that she just stood there holding the receiver. Then she hung up and dialed again. "Hello. This is Henry Rawson. I am not at home at the moment . . ." the voice repeated.

"I know. I know," said DeDe impatiently as her father's recorded voice continued. The signal sounded. Again DeDe was speechless. It was strange to hear her father's voice and not be able to speak to him. Then she hurried. "Dad, it's me, DeDe. You know my number, but in case you forgot it's 555-6867. Don't forget area code 201. My class is giving a play next week. It's not really a play, but Mrs. Sussman decided to make it into a play instead of working on something else.

Besides, another class is doing a play for Thanksgiving. And I—" The tone sounded again.

"Did I use up all of my time?" DeDe asked the telephone. There was no answer.

"Dad has a telephone answering machine," DeDe told her mother. Mrs. Rawson had just walked into the kitchen. "I think I used up all my time. I better call again."

DeDe dialed and listened as the voice said, "Hello. This is Henry Rawson. I am not at home . . ."

When the message finished, DeDe picked up where she had left off. "Anyhow. I'm going to be Marie Antoinette and I have a fake head and I hope you can come." She hung up before she realized that she hadn't told the machine who she was the second time. She also hadn't said when the play was and how she could go back to the city with her father afterward.

"If your father comes, do you want me to stay home?" Mrs. Rawson asked DeDe.

"Stay home? Why should you stay home? Do you have to work that day?"

"Well, it might be embarrassing for you to

have your parents at school together when they are divorced," said Mrs. Rawson.

DeDe hadn't thought about that. Suppose her parents had a fight in front of everyone at school? Or suppose they didn't talk to each other?

She told her worries to Aldo at lunch the next day. "Do you think it's okay for both of my parents to come to our play?"

"Why not?" said Aldo.

"They hardly talk to each other."

"No one is supposed to talk during an assembly," Aldo pointed out. "The only time you can open your mouth is to recite the Pledge of Allegiance and to sing 'America.' If your parents started talking, they would probably be sent to Mrs. O'Reilly's office and have to stay after school."

DeDe giggled at the thought of her parents pulling a detention. Two detentions and you had to bring a note from your parents.

So it was decided that both Mr. and Mrs. Rawson were to come to the assembly. "I'm looking forward to seeing you in the play," DeDe's father told her when he, and not his machine, spoke to her the next evening.

"Actually, you won't be able to see me too well," DeDe explained. Her turtleneck would be covering her head part of the time. "But you can hear my voice," she promised.

The day of the play was crisp and cold. DeDe had her overnight bag packed before she left the house for school. She decided it would be safer if she was prepared to leave immediately after school. She no longer had daydreams about her parents getting back together. A year ago she had felt differently.

DeDe's class was fidgeting. Everyone was worried about whether they would remember their lines. They had made a big map of France as the backdrop for the play. They couldn't set up anything until after lunch because the school auditorium also served as the lunchroom. It was called the cafetorium.

After lunch the tables were folded against the wall, and the floor was quickly mopped. Folding chairs were arranged along the back and sides for teachers and parents. Then the classes marched into the cafetorium and sat on the floor. It was still a little damp. DeDe looked around her as she marched in, trying to find her parents. She hoped her father wouldn't be late.

A chord was played and everyone stood up. "We will now recite the Pledge of Allegiance," said Mrs. O'Reilly. Boys and girls and parents all turned to face the flag. DeDe was glad that her voice sounded normal. Her mouth felt dry and she thought that no sound would come out at all. After the pledge, they sang "America." Some parents sang very loudly, and it covered those who couldn't carry a tune. Last year the class play had been a musical, and DeDe had had to sing the "Song of the Merry Leaves" with three other girls who were also trees. Her father had said they'd all sounded like they had Dutch elm disease.

Finally, after a welcome to the parents from Mrs. O'Reilly, it was time for the play to begin.

Aldo stood up and faced the audience.

"Bone Jur," he said. Then he explained that he had greeted everyone in French. "And now you are going to meet some important people in French history," he said. That was the signal for Louis XVI, Napoleon, de Gaulle, and all the others to march to the back of the stage. Quickly, they picked up their props and lined up to wait for their turn.

The boy who was ahead of DeDe was named Louis, and he had been assigned Louis XVI. DeDe was afraid she would be teased when she had first discovered that she was supposed to be married to him. But everyone had been so interested in her guillotined head that they hadn't noticed the marriage part. As for Louis, he had lost his head during the French Revolution, too, and he was upset that he didn't have a papier-mâché one of his own to show off.

Louis finished his speech, and DeDe went forward to give hers. Almost immediately she saw her father. He had a seat at the end of one of the rows in a chair meant for a teacher. He smiled at her, and DeDe had trouble keeping a straight face. Marie Antoinette was about to lose her head. She could not smile. Not even at her father. DeDe had to keep the dignity of royalty. That's what Mrs. Sussman had said.

"I am Marie Antoinette," DeDe told the

audience. "I am wearing a white wig that was the style in the eighteenth century. I am the Queen of France and I am very rich. When the poor people were hungry and wanted bread, I told them to eat cake." DeDe shook her head as she spoke so that her mother's long earrings would swing back and forth. She had a beauty mark painted under her left eye. She was also wearing eye shadow and lipstick. As she shook her head, she was careful not to shake off the wig her mother had helped her to make out of cotton. It was attached to her own hair with about a hundred bobby pins, but she was still scared it would fall off.

"The poor people didn't have any cake and they became angry," DeDe continued. "They stormed the palace and captured my husband and me. We were put into prison, and the French Revolution began."

Then came the part that DeDe liked best. "One morning I was brought before the guillotine. I lay down on the ground," said DeDe, bending over carefully and pulling at her turtleneck shirt as she spoke. "The knife came down fast." Then DeDe whipped out the papier-mâché head she'd been holding behind her back. She held it up high for everyone to see. "My head was chopped off!" she shouted. It was the most dramatic moment of the entire production.

When they had made the head, Mrs. Rawson had poked a hole in the bottom for DeDe's thumb to fit inside. That way, she could hold the head with one hand without dropping it. Now DeDe's thumb accidentally slipped out of the hole. Her real head was inside her shirt, so she couldn't see. The head slipped out of her hand and bounced across the stage. Nothing like this had ever happened during rehearsals. "I lost my head!" DeDe cried out as the audience roared with laughter.

DeDe was led off the stage by the boy who came next. He was playing the part of Robespierre, and he was supposed to help her since her head was still hidden inside the shirt. As she walked off, there was another wild cheer. It was not until she was backstage that she found out what happened. "Robespierre

kicked your head like a soccer ball," Aldo explained. "It was the best part of the show."

When the play and the assembly, too, had concluded, everyone was supposed to march out. Only DeDe's class remained in the cafetorium. Mrs. Sussman had brought a cake, and there was a bowl of pink punch for the children and their parents to share. DeDe saw her mother talking to Mrs. Sossi. They were probably exchanging vegetable recipes.

"Did you like the play?" DeDe asked her father.

"Sure," he said, hugging her. "It was a real flesh-and-blood affair."

"You mean because I lost my head?"

"Because you need to have a flesh-and-blood relation in the play to be able to sit through it," explained Mr. Rawson.

DeDe introduced her father to Mrs. Sussman. "I came all the way from New York to see this play," he said.

"Do you work in the city?" the teacher asked.

"I work and live there," said DeDe's father.

"Oh, yes, of course. I forgot," said Mrs. Sussman. "I'm glad you were able to come. DeDe outdid herself with that head."

Mrs. Rawson came toward them and shook hands with DeDe's teacher. Other parents milled around, so you really couldn't tell who was with whom and who was talking to whom.

"Do we have to wait for three o'clock?" Mr. Rawson asked.

"No, you may leave now if you'd like," Mrs. Sussman answered. "There are rewards to the theatrical life," said Mr. Rawson, taking DeDe by the arm.

Mrs. Rawson followed and got into her car while DeDe got into her father's. Mr. Rawson's car was clean inside and out and started instantly.

Mrs. Rawson's car started, too, so they all arrived at the house at the same time. But now it didn't matter if her parents talked or didn't talk. Now there was no one to see except Cookie.

"Would you like a cup of coffee?" Mrs. Rawson offered. DeDe could tell that she wasn't comfortable.

"No, thanks," said Mr. Rawson. "We might as well get started right away and miss the traffic. Come on, DeDe. We've got tickets to a real play this evening."

As they drove toward the city, he told her that he had found a new restaurant he wanted to try out. "Good," said DeDe. After eating so many vegetables in so many disguises, she felt she was suffering from an overdose of vitamins. She hoped this new place would serve good old French fries.

"What play are we going to see?" DeDe asked.

"It's a surprise," said her father. "But I have to warn you, there won't be any flying heads."

Eight

Thanksgiving

The weekend had gotten off to a great start, and DeDe's spirits had stayed high until just before it was time for her to go home. That's when Mr. Rawson had told her that he had to leave on another business trip to California. She would not be able to spend her next scheduled weekend with him. And worst of all, that weekend was Thanksgiving.

Walking to school with Aldo on Monday

morning, DeDe looked at the kindergarten windows. They were decorated with cutouts of turkeys that the little children had made.

"I wish I was back in kindergarten drawing turkeys again," DeDe said. Kindergarten was B.D.

"Hey," said Aldo. "You don't think I would hang around with a little kid in kindergarten, do you?"

DeDe shrugged miserably.

"So what's your father going to do in California?" Aldo asked.

"His company is opening a new office, and he's going there to arrange things. I wish Thanksgiving was over already," DeDe sighed. "I'm tired of looking at those old paper turkeys."

"Oh, well," said Aldo. "You'll soon be seeing Christmas decorations instead. They go up the second Thanksgiving is over."

DeDe nodded. She wondered where she would spend Christmas vacation. That was an even longer holiday than Thanksgiving.

"Maybe you could have Thanksgiving dinner at my house?" Aldo offered.

DeDe shook her head. She always enjoyed eating at Aldo's house, but Thanksgiving was a family holiday. She didn't want to spend it with someone else's family. "My mother and I will do something special," said DeDe. "Thanks anyhow."

There was still a week until Thanksgiving. DeDe waited to see what her mother would suggest. But when she didn't say anything, DeDe asked, "Could we plan a Thanksgiving dinner here and have company?"

"Oh, no," said Mrs. Rawson. "I still remember my last attempt at playing hostess."

"Could Grandma and Grandpa come?" asked DeDe. That would make the holiday really special.

"You've forgotten that they went to Florida. They rented an apartment there until March."

DeDe had forgotten. "Then it's just you and me," she said sadly.

"It could be worse," said Mrs. Rawson. "Before it was just me, and now I've got you."

DeDe looked at her mother. She hadn't asked herself if her mother would mind if she had gone off to visit her father. And she really hadn't thought about what her mother would do all alone on Thanksgiving.

"I know," said Mrs. Rawson. "Let's have dinner at a restaurant."

DeDe had always wondered what kind of people ate in restaurants on Thanksgiving. Orphans? Divorced people? People without any family or friends? It would probably be awful. Of course, she admitted, if she had been with her father she would almost certainly have eaten in a restaurant. But somehow that was different. DeDe didn't expect her father to cook his own holiday turkey.

"I don't want to eat out," DeDe pouted. "You always make me order the kiddie specials. I don't want the Humpty Dumpty Dinner or the Bo Peep Platter for Thanksgiving."

"Of course not," agreed Mrs. Rawson. "You can order anything you want."

That was their plan for the holiday. But DeDe was not happy about it.

On Thanksgiving morning, she watched the big parade on television. She sat on the floor with Cookie by her side and wondered what was wrong. She had watched the parade every year since she was a baby, but today something wasn't right. It didn't feel like Thanksgiving at all. "I guess I'm getting too old to watch this," she told Cookie as she switched the dial on the TV, trying without success to find something else.

"It doesn't feel like Thanksgiving," DeDe complained to her mother.

Her mother nodded. "It's the smell."

"What smell?"

"This is the first year that we don't have a turkey roasting in the oven. The house doesn't smell like Thanksgiving," Mrs. Rawson explained. "We should invent a spray. You know how they sell rose and lemon deodorant sprays to make your house smell good. We should invent a turkey spray for people who don't roast a turkey on Thanksgiving. We could make a fortune."

But it wasn't just the smell that was wrong, DeDe knew. It was the absence of her father. This was the first Thanksgiving A.D. It wasn't something to be thankful about.

DeDe had an idea and went to the telephone. Quickly, she dialed her father's apartment in the city. The phone rang two times before there was a click and she heard her father's voice. "Hello. This is Henry Rawson. I am not at home at the moment, but I will return your call as soon as possible. At the signal, please leave your name, phone number, and a brief message. You will have twenty seconds."

DeDe sniffed and blinked her eyes. She had thought that hearing her father's voice would make her feel better. But it just made her feel worse. She hung up without saying anything. It didn't really matter. He wouldn't be home for another full week.

Mrs. Rawson had made a reservation at the Homestead Restaurant for two o'clock. At one, DeDe took off her jeans and started to put on her velvet party dress. She felt silly putting on a fancy dress to eat with her mother. She went into her mother's bedroom and saw that she was putting on her silk print dress.

"Look," her mother said proudly. "All those salads have helped me lose weight. This dress never fit so well before."

DeDe shrugged. Even though she had once

been concerned about her mother getting fat, she was feeling too sorry for herself to care about that now.

She looked down at Cookie, who had been following her around. "I want Cookie to eat with us," she told her mother.

"The Homestead would never be the same," said Mrs. Rawson. "You know dogs aren't allowed in restaurants."

"Cookie isn't just a dog. She's family. And this is a family holiday," DeDe sulked. "If she can't come with us, I don't want to go."

"Maybe we can bring home a treat for her," offered Mrs. Rawson. "A doggie bag."

"I think a whole family should be together on a holiday," said DeDe. "It isn't right to leave Cookie here alone."

"Cookie doesn't know it's a holiday. She's probably wondering why you are home from school."

"I don't care. I want her to come with us," said DeDe.

"Cookie is staying home," said Mrs. Rawson firmly. "You and I are going out. Now that's final."

DeDe started to sob. "Cookie, you know I love you even if I go away."

"DeDe, stop making a soap opera out of a this," warned Mrs. Rawson. She handed DeDe a tissue for her nose. "Let's go or we'll miss our reservation."

DeDe slumped down in the front seat of the car. She didn't want any dinner at the Homestead. In the Pilgrims' day, animals and people all lived together and they ate together, too.

"You must be very hungry," said Mrs. Rawson as they drove along. "You hardly had any breakfast at all."

"I'm not hungry," DeDe growled.

After that Mrs. Rawson kept her eyes on the road. The Homestead parking lot was almost full, but there was a space near the front. Mrs. Rawson slowly edged into it, but she didn't allow enough room on the right side.

"Oh, dear," Mrs. Rawson sighed. She backed out slowly and tried to readjust her angle before pulling in.

Her mother pulled into and out of the

space three times before she was finally able to make it. "Dad would have just zipped into this space," DeDe told her mother as she got out of the car.

"What can I tell you? I'm not perfect," snapped Mrs. Rawson.

"You can say that again," said DeDe. She was feeling angry, and angry words kept coming out of her mouth.

Mrs. Rawson didn't say anything. "What are you going to order?" she asked DeDe after they were seated.

DeDe looked down at the menu. "I'll take a broiled lobster."

"For Thanksgiving dinner?" asked Mrs. Rawson. "The Pilgrim fathers didn't eat lobster."

"I don't care about the Pilgrim fathers. My father eats lobster, and I want one, too."

"It's the most expensive dish on the menu. Are you sure you wouldn't prefer turkey?"

"You promised I could have anything I wanted," DeDe reminded her mother.

"Yes," agreed her mother. "I'd forgotten that you've developed such expensive tastes."

A family was seated across from the Rawsons: a mother, a father, a boy of seven, a girl of four, and two white-haired grandparents. DeDe looked at them enviously. They looked like a television commercial for soap or tomato sauce or something. She wished she were a part of that family.

DeDe leaned sideways in her chair, trying to hear what they were saying. Suddenly the mother turned to the grandmother and in a low voice hissed, "Oh, mother. Do be quiet." DeDe sat stunned. She felt betrayed. Those were not the words she had expected to hear from this "perfect family." Her eyes filled with tears for about the third time that afternoon. Did she sound that mean when she spoke to her mother?

The waitress came to their table. Mrs. Rawson ordered the turkey special for herself, and then she turned to DeDe.

"Me, too," DeDe whispered.

After the waitress left, DeDe said, "I can't bring lobster shells home for Cookie." Then she smiled at her mother. "I'm sorry, Mom," she said.

"So am I," her mother said. "It's not your fault that you're part of a modern statistic."

"What do you mean?" asked DeDe.

"More than half of all marriages end in divorce these days," her mother replied. "But children grow up anyway, and divorced people do go on with their lives—even if it may seem to you that I'm not doing such a good job of it right now. Everyone's life has it's ups and downs," she said. "Sometimes it just takes a little longer to bounce up again." Her mother reached under the table and squeezed DeDe's hand. "Let's eat," she said as the waitress put the food on the table.

They had fruit cocktail, roast turkey and stuffing, candied sweet potatoes, string beans, and cranberry sauce. Mrs. Rawson turned down dessert, even though it came with the dinner. "My dress fits too well for me to risk it getting tight again. Besides," she said, "I am very full."

DeDe was full, too. But that was no reason to turn down apple pie with a scoop of chocolate ice cream.

"That was good," said DeDe.

"And no dishes to wash," said her mother, smiling.

When Mrs. Rawson paid the waitress, she said something to her quietly. The woman nodded. In a few minutes, she returned with a paper bag. DeDe peeked inside and saw two big steak bones for Cookie.

"Our dog is part of our family, so we didn't want to forget her today," said Mrs. Rawson.

"Her name is Cookie," said DeDe. "But she eats everything. Even stuffed cabbage."

DeDe took her mother's hand as they left the restaurant. The family at the next table was still eating. They looked like the perfect happy family. But looks could be deceiving. DeDe and her mother and Cookie were a family, too.

Nine

DeDe
Makes a Plan

Thanksgiving weekend ended with a long-distance telephone call for DeDe. It was her father calling from California to wish her a good holiday. DeDe didn't tell him that his tape machine had spoken to her on Thursday. She now thought that had been a babyish thing to do.

Mr. Rawson had good news. He had made arrangements for DeDe to spend her Christmas vacation in California with him.

"Do you really mean it?" she asked.

"Absolutely!" her father promised.

So now DeDe was eagerly looking ahead to Christmas. It tickled her that when her mother would be going to bed at eleven o'clock at night, it would only be eight o'clock in California and DeDe would still be up. But the thought of her mother alone in the house (though Cookie would be staying home, too) made DeDe sad. If only her mother had as many new friends as her father. DeDe decided it was up to her to find a companion for her mother before she went away. But the only members of the male sex that DeDe knew personally were the boys in her class at school. She thought about the teachers. Most were women, but there were two men on the staff at Woodside Elementary School. There was Mr. Ellis, who taught band, but he was married. His wife always attended the student concerts, and it was said that she had a pair of special earplugs for those occasions.

The other male teacher was Mr. Evans. He taught shop. He might not be married. DeDe decided to find out.

The fifth grade had shop twice a week. DeDe's class went on Wednesdays and Fridays at eleven o'clock. On the Wednesday after Thanksgiving, DeDe waited impatiently for Mrs. Sussman to send them to the shop room. They were still working on their birdhouses. It wasn't usually DeDe's favorite activity, but today she greeted Mr. Evans with a big smile.

"Hi," she said. "Do you think I can finish my birdhouse today?"

Mr. Evans leaned over to examine the pieces of wood that DeDe had nailed together. "They should be sanded a little smoother," he suggested. As he leaned forward, DeDe looked carefully at his hands. He wasn't wearing a wedding ring. That was a good sign.

DeDe took a deep breath. "Do you teach your own kids how to make things?" she asked Mr. Evans. She hoped he wouldn't think it was funny that she was asking him such a personal question. But how else was she going to find out if he was married?

"I don't have any children of my own," said

Mr. Evans. "But I give a mini-course to the Boy Scouts."

DeDe nodded. So far, so good. He didn't have any children. But did he have a wife? She took another breath. "Is your wife good at making things, too?" she asked.

"I don't have a wife yet," said Mr. Evans, walking off to examine the birdhouses of the students on the other side of the worktable.

No wife yet. Did that mean he had a girl-friend? Did it mean he was engaged? DeDe wasn't sure what Mr. Evans's answer meant. But at least he wasn't married. She could proceed with her plan.

After she sanded her birdhouse, she went looking for the paint. They could choose red, yellow, or blue. DeDe selected yellow and brought a can of paint and a brush over to the table. She wondered if the color you chose mattered to the birds.

Painting didn't take much time but now the house had to dry, and that would take another day. DeDe was too impatient to wait.

When the class was leaving the room at the end of the hour, DeDe hung behind. "Mr.

Evans," she said. "I want to give this bird-house to my mother for her birthday today. Could I come and pick it up at three o'clock instead of waiting until Friday when we have shop again?"

"The paint will still be damp," Mr. Evans warned DeDe.

"If it isn't dry, I'll carry it home very carefully," DeDe assured the shop teacher. "See you at three," she called as she rushed down the hall after her classmates.

"How come you were talking with Mr. Evans?" asked Traci when they were back in their seats.

"He's going to let me take my birdhouse home early because it's my mother's birthday," DeDe explained.

"Again?" asked Traci.

"Not exactly," said DeDe. "But this was part of her present." DeDe was beginning to believe it really was her mother's birthday.

At three o'clock, she pulled every book out of her desk, including a few she didn't need to take home. She had already borrowed a couple of Traci's books, too. She had also gone to the school library and taken out three of the thickest books she could find.

"How are you going to make it home with all those books?" asked Aldo as DeDe staggered out of the door. "Do you want me to help?"

"No thanks, not today. I have a plan. But could I borrow your social studies textbook?"

"Are you nuts?" asked Aldo. "You've already got two copies, and we don't even have any social studies homework."

"It's all part of my plan," said DeDe mysteriously. "I can't explain now. One book is Traci's and one is mine. I really need yours, too."

"You've cracked up," said Aldo, handing over his book.

"I'll tell you all about it tomorrow," said DeDe, adding Aldo's fat textbook to her pile. She carried the books in her arms with her chin resting on the top to help balance them.

Slowly, she made her way down the hall to the shop room.

Mr. Evans was sweeping up sawdust and shavings from the floor.

"Hi," called DeDe. It wasn't easy to speak with her chin on the books. She couldn't open her mouth very wide. "I've come for the birdhouse."

"Just a minute," said Mr. Evans. He went over to the row of painted houses and looked for the yellow one with DeDe's label.

"How in the world are you going to get this home?" he asked.

"I'll manage," DeDe gasped. "I'm very strong."

"You may be strong, but you only have two arms," said the teacher. "Aren't any of your friends going in your direction?"

"No," said DeDe, trying to make her voice sound forlorn.

Mr. Evans rested the yellow birdhouse on top of the huge pile of books. DeDe could no longer rest her chin on the pile. In fact, the pile of books and the house now reached over her head and blocked her vision.

"Careful. Don't get hit by a car," said Mr. Evans as he returned to his sweeping.

DeDe didn't move. Her plan was for Mr. Evans to offer her a ride home. The only problem was that he didn't know that he was part of the plan, so he kept on sweeping.

"Do you need help cleaning up?" offered DeDe.

"The clean-up monitor in my last class was called to the office," explained Mr. Evans. "I don't like to leave the shop a mess."

"I'll help," said DeDe, putting the books and the birdhouse down on one of the worktables. She rushed to get the dustpan before Mr. Evans could refuse her assistance.

Together they finished the job. "Thanks very much," Mr. Evans said.

"My mother always says one good turn deserves another," said DeDe. Her mother had never said any such thing, but she had heard it somewhere and it seemed appropriate to the situation. Maybe Mr. Evans would now give her a ride home.

"That's right. I let you take the birdhouse home early," agreed Mr. Evans. "It came out quite well. I'm sure your mother will like it."

DeDe had forgotten that Mr. Evans had already given his good turn of the day. "Well, I hope she likes it and the birds like it, too.

If I can make it home," Dede said, carefully dropping all her books but not the birdhouse.

"Here," said Mr. Evans. "You'll balance them better if the larger books are on the bottom. He started piling the books into DeDe's arms. "DeDe," said Mr. Evans in a puzzled tone, "why do you have three copies of the same book?"

"Oh," said DeDe, searching for an answer. It had never occurred to her that he might notice. "I'm doing a special project." She thought fast. "I'm checking if these books are really the same. Sometimes they make little changes in the text."

Mr. Evans scratched his head. "I'm glad I'm teaching shop," he said.

He bent to pick up another book from the floor. "I didn't know you were such a scholar." When he wasn't looking, DeDe opened her arms, and the books went crashing to the floor a second time. "Oh, dear," she sighed mournfully. "I don't know how I'll ever make it home."

"Tell you what," said Mr. Evans, looking at

his watch. "I'll give you a lift on my way home."

"Oh, would you?" DeDe pretended to be surprised. "That's so nice of you."

Mr. Evans put on his jacket and helped her carry some of the books. "I just have to sign out," he said, stopping at the school office. DeDe leaned against the wall outside, waiting. Her plan was working perfectly after all. I ought to go on the stage, she thought, forgetting her mishap with Marie Antoinette's head.

Oh, would you? That's so nice of you, she had said to Mr. Evans, as if she hadn't been thinking of that ever since she first hatched the plan.

I wonder how my name would look in lights?

Ten

More Surprises

Mr. Evans, DeDe, thirteen school books, and one sticky yellow birdhouse all squeezed into the teacher's car.

It occurred to DeDe as they drove that for her plan to work she had to let Mr. Evans know that her mother was unmarried, too. She tried to think of the best way to word this. Finally she said, "The reason I was in such a rush to take this home is that I want to make sure my mother has a happy birthday. She just got divorced, you see."

Mr. Evans didn't say anything, so DeDe didn't know if he saw or not. When they reached her house, Mr. Evans didn't turn off the motor. "Won't you come in?" asked DeDe. He *had* to come in. That was the most important part of her plan. "You could have some milk and cookies," she offered. It was the sort of thing she would have said to someone her own age. She hoped it didn't sound too silly. She didn't know what teachers had for after-school snacks. Maybe he wanted a martini or something.

"I think I better get along," said Mr. Evans. "You should be able to make it from here."

"I'd really like you to meet my mother. I told her what a great shop teacher I have," said DeDe, hoping her mother wouldn't give her away. She had never, as far as she could remember, mentioned her shop teacher at home.

"Well, all right. Just for a minute, then," said Mr. Evans reluctantly as he turned off the car's ignition. He took a few of the books off DeDe's lap and got out of the car. DeDe sighed with relief. She had made it this far. Now it was up to her mother to charm the shop teacher. She knew for sure that her mother was home. She never worked on Wednesdays.

DeDe led the way to the door and rang the bell. She had too much to carry, even with Mr. Evans's help, to use her key. She could hear Cookie barking inside.

After a long pause, the door opened, and Cookie and Mrs. Rawson appeared. Cookie looked the same as ever, but Mrs. Rawson's head was wrapped in a towel and her face was covered with a thick, dark paste. She looked like something out of a horror movie.

"Yikes!" gasped DeDe over Cookie's barks. "What's wrong with you, Mom?"

"Nothing's wrong," answered her mother sharply. "I just made myself a facial out of the leftover avocado in our last vegetable delivery. I wasn't expecting company."

"This is Mr. Evans, my shop teacher," said DeDe, introducing her mother. "He brought

me home because I had so much to carry to-day."

"That was very nice of you," said Mrs. Rawson stiffly. "Do come in."

"I think I'd better get home," said Mr. Evans, staring at DeDe's mother. He looked like he'd never seen such a sight.

"This is for you," DeDe said, handing her mother the sticky yellow birdhouse. She hoped it would distract everyone. "I made it for you at school."

"It's very interesting," said Mrs. Rawson. "A jewelry box shaped like a house."

"It's not a jewelry box," said DeDe, hoping Mr. Evans wasn't upset. "It's a birdhouse."

"Happy birthday, Mrs. Rawson," said Mr. Evans.

"Happy birthday?" asked DeDe's mother.

"Yes," said DeDe, nodding her head vigorously. "Happy birthday, Mom."

"What are you talking about?" asked Mrs. Rawson. "My birthday was last month. You don't have to age me any faster than nature is doing."

Just then the telephone rang.

"It was nice meeting you," said Mr. Evans. "I'll see *you* at school, DeDe," he said as he backed out the door.

Mrs. Rawson went to answer it, leaving DeDe to ponder the failure of all her efforts. How could she ever have guessed that her mother would choose today to experiment with a vegetable facial? She had never done that before. Even if Mr. Evans had come the day the clothes dryer broke, as Aldo had done, it would have been better. At least he might even have known how to fix the broken dryer, and Mrs. Rawson would have been grateful to him. And why did her mother have to tell Mr. Evans that today wasn't her birthday?

Mrs. Rawson was so distracted after she hung up the telephone that she didn't mention Mr. Evans or the fact that it wasn't her birthday. Instead she said, "That was Mrs. Sossi. She's coming over."

"Today isn't a vegetable delivery day, is it?" asked DeDe.

"No. She didn't say what she wanted. She said she would explain when she got here." Mrs. Rawson removed the towel from her head. "I'm going to dry my hair and wash my face. Listen for the door bell," she said.

DeDe wondered why Aldo's mother was coming. She didn't have long to think about it. In five minutes, Mrs. Sossi was there. Karen was with her.

"Karen told me about your planters, and I wanted to see them myself," Mrs. Sossi explained. "A handmade planter would make a wonderful Christmas present."

"I haven't made any in over a year," said Mrs. Rawson, showing the various pots that she had around the house.

"Aren't they great?" asked Karen.

"They certainly are," agreed Mrs. Sossi. "How much do you sell them for?" she asked.

"I used to get twenty-five dollars apiece," said Mrs. Rawson.

"Could you make me three?" asked Mrs. Sossi. "No, make it four. I want one for myself, too. I especially like this one," she said, pointing to Karen's favorite with the dangling earrings.

"Hey, that's a hundred dollars," said DeDe, who had been listening to the conversation. Imagine Mrs. Sossi wanting to spend a hundred dollars on her mother's planters.

"You could make a lot of money with these," said Mrs. Sossi. "I'm sure that other people I know will want them once they've seen mine. We all just run in and out on vegetable pickup days, and no one ever has time to look around. You should have a special show here in the house one evening and take orders."

When Mrs. Sossi and Karen left, DeDe's mother went down to the basement to check her kiln. The pottery oven had been sitting unused for many months.

"What a wonderful surprise," said Mrs. Rawson, coming back upstairs. "Imagine getting four orders, just like that, out of nowhere. DeDe, you brought me good luck!"

DeDe blushed. With all her scheming and plotting, this was one thing that she had never even considered.

"You shouldn't be surprised," said DeDe, although she was surprised herself. "Your planters are terrific. I bet they would even sell them at the department store if you brought some to show them."

"What do you say we go out and celebrate?" asked Mrs. Rawson. "Tonight I could even afford to buy you a lobster dinner!"

DeDe weighed the offer. "You know what I would like even better?"

"Roast beef?" asked her mother. "Or a juicy steak?"

"No. Let's eat dinner at home and save money to get the dishwasher fixed."

"Good idea," agreed Mrs. Rawson. "I'm going to need all my spare time for working on these planters. I won't have time to help you with the dishes."

She picked up the birdhouse. "If I make some money, maybe we can even get someone to patch the ceiling and paint the living room."

"Yellow?" asked DeDe.

"That's a nice color for a birdhouse," said DeDe's mother, "but I think we'll pick a quieter shade for our house."

It was a fine evening, and the subject of birthdays and Mr. Evans never came up. Not even once.

Eleven

Another Birthday Present

*E*ven though it was the holiday season and DeDe's mother was working long hours in the department store, she found time to work on her planters. Several people in the vegetable club had placed orders after Mrs. Sossi told them about the planters. Mrs. Rawson bought a new supply of clay and paints. The more she pounded and shaped the clay, the happier she seemed. She even started making new planters that were children's heads with smiling faces and missing teeth. She was planning to put an ad in the local newspaper after the holidays. For now she had as much work as she could handle.

"Why don't you quit your job?" DeDe asked her mother as the orders kept coming in.

"Maybe I will," said Mrs. Rawson. "But I'm afraid these sales will peak. Soon everyone in Woodside will have a Rawson planter. There won't be any customers left."

"But after Woodside you can try Teaneck and River Edge and Summit and Haworth," said DeDe, naming nearby communities.

"The best thing, even better than the money," said Mrs. Rawson, "is that this is something I really enjoy doing."

DeDe knew what her mother meant. She and Aldo would sometimes try to make little figures out of bits of clay. Aldo tried to make his cats Peabody and Poughkeepsie and DeDe tried to make a dog like Cookie. It was fun, but none of their attempts resembled their models at all. DeDe may have inherited her teeth from her mother, but she hadn't inherited any of her talent.

"Your mother is really super!" Aldo said

one day. "She can make great things. She made you that Marie Antoinette head for school. Even the vegetables look more special in your house than mine." DeDe's mother had drawn funny faces on some odd-shaped squash and made a centerpiece for the dining room table.

DeDe had always been proud of her father's success at work. But until Aldo pointed it out to her, she had hardly been aware of her mother's talents.

"Is this a weekend when you visit your father?" Aldo asked DeDe. With all the trips her father had been taking recently, odd and even dates didn't mean much anymore.

"I'm going to be here in Woodside," said DeDe. "But next weekend I'm flying to California." She was really looking forward to her long holiday with her father.

"We're going to visit my cousin Marco this weekend," said Aldo. "But I have two tickets to the musical *Guys and Dolls* at the high school. Elaine got them because she helped paint the scenery for the show. Do you want them?"

114

"How much do they cost?" asked DeDe. As usual she was broke.

"Nothing," said Aldo. "Elaine got them for free, and I wouldn't charge you."

"Perfect," said DeDe. "I'll take my mother."

"Happy birthday," said DeDe, handing her mother the pair of tickets later that afternoon.

"Happy birthday? Again?" asked Mrs. Rawson. "At this rate, I'm becoming ancient."

"Well. It can be an early Christmas present, then," said DeDe. She already had a picture frame she had made in shop hidden in the closet to give her mother for Christmas.

The high-school auditorium was packed that evening. It looked like everyone in Woodside was there. DeDe hoped that the other people had paid for their tickets because the program said that the money raised from the evening's performance would go to the Woodside High School Scholarship Fund.

The entire cast of the show was made up of teachers, some of whose names DeDe recognized from her elementary school. The other teachers came from the middle school and the high school. A boy behind DeDe was laughing with his friends because their English teacher, Mr. Dunn, was playing the lead, Sky Masterson.

The sets looked as good as any DeDe had seen at the Broadway shows her father had taken her to in the past year. She squeezed her mother's hand. "This is going to be good," she said as the conductor led the orchestra into the overture.

During the intermission, DeDe and her mother got up to stretch their legs. "Hello," said a voice behind DeDe's back. It was Mr. Evans.

"Hi," said DeDe. She was a little embarrassed to meet him face-to-face with her mother. "How come you aren't in the play?" she asked.

"I helped build the sets," he said.

"Very professional-looking," said Mrs. Rawson.

Mr. Evans smiled.

"We put the birdhouse out in our yard," DeDe said.

"Any birds move in yet?" Mr. Evans asked.

"No," said DeDe. "We have to wait until spring."

"Maybe we'll put an ad in the newspaper and let the birds know it's available," said Mrs. Rawson, smiling.

The lights began to blink. "Time for the second act," said DeDe.

"May I drive you home?" asked Mr. Evans.

Wow, DeDe thought. I didn't even plan this one.

"That's nice of you," said Mrs. Rawson. "But we have our car."

If ever there was a time to abandon a car, this was it, DeDe thought. She could have kicked her mother. They could have gotten their car out of the school parking lot the next morning.

But then Mrs. Rawson said, "Why don't you follow us home and have a cup of coffee?"

So it was all right. "I'd love to," said Mr. Evans.

They got into their seats just as the conductor was taking his place again. The second act was beginning.

The rest of the evening went just as DeDe would have planned it, only better. The play ended, and they returned home, followed by Mr. Evans. He stayed for one hour and had two cups of coffee and three oatmeal cookies. The cookies came out of a package. DeDe thought, if only her mother was a great baker like Aldo's sister. But Mr. Evans didn't seem to mind that the cookies weren't home-baked. He admired the planters in the living room, waiting for her mother's customers to pick them up. When he left, he said, "May I call you?"

"I'd like that," Mrs. Rawson said.

"Do you like him?" DeDe asked her mother as soon as the door closed behind Mr. Evans.

"DeDe. I hardly know him," her mother said. "Don't try to marry me off," she added. "I may marry again someday. I don't know. But just remember. Whatever happens, it will be all right. And you don't have to arrange things. They'll arrange themselves."

"How do you mean?" asked DeDe.

"I know that you arranged for me to meet Mr. Evans. But I'm a grown-up. I can find my own friends."

"But you didn't," DeDe pointed out.

"True. But I wasn't ready to then. Now I am. Anyway, some things have to happen naturally. Some things have to be arranged."

"Like what?" asked DeDe.

"Like your teeth, for example. If we left them to grown in naturally, they wouldn't be straight. Braces will help arrange your teeth properly. But other things, like relationships, can't be arranged. There are no wires or rubber bands that can hold a marriage together, or hook up two strangers. People have to do that for themselves. Sometimes they succeed and sometimes they don't. And either way, life goes on."

"Okay," said DeDe. "I get the message already."

"I have another message for you," said her mother. "It's way past your bedtime."

"In California, it's only nine o'clock."

"True. But you're not in California yet," said Mrs. Rawson, kissing her good night.

DeDe went upstairs and put on her pajamas. In the bathroom, she washed her face and hands. Then she brushed her teeth carefully, as Dr. Curry had shown her. It was

quiet in the bathroom. You couldn't hear anyone brushing their teeth next door.

When she finished rinsing her mouth, she put on her headgear and bit down. She looked in the mirror and wriggled her nose at her Martian appearance. Oh, well, she thought. Nine months were already behind her. She would survive braces, like she had survived the divorce. One day she would be A.B., after braces, as well as A.D., after divorce.

"Good night," she said to Cookie as she climbed into bed. The dog settled down on the rug in her usual spot.

When she was almost asleep, another thought passed through DeDe's mind. Wouldn't it be wonderful if Mr. Evans liked brussels sprouts?

And then, in another minute, DeDe and Cookie were both fast asleep.